The Wishing Shell

An Old Tale from Nepal
Retold by May Nelson
Illustrated by Xiangyi Mo and Jingwen Wang

Nepal

When Tensing looks up at the majestic mountains that tower above his small village in Nepal, he knows there must be magic in the air. Why else would people come from so many faraway countries to explore the snowy slopes of the world's highest mountains?

In this tale from Nepal, we learn that showing *compassion*, even to the humblest of creatures, can bring rich rewards and happiness.

compassion concern for others in need

Kauda and his father lived in a little wooden hut in a village in the mountains of Nepal. They were happy together, but they were very poor. All day long, they worked in the rice fields, tending the crops. It was tiring work, and their backs ached from bending over. When they stopped to rest, it made them happy to see the snow sparkling on the mountain peaks high above them. The air was pure and clean, and they could hear the birds singing.

One day, Kauda said, "Father, I must leave our village to go and seek my fortune. If I'm lucky, I may bring back some riches for us to share, and you will not have to work so hard."

Kauda's father hugged his son and gave him three hundred rupees that he had been able to save. "May luck go with you," he said.

rupee   the unit of money used in Nepal

Kauda set out down the track and before long came to another small village, where he saw a man kicking a cat.

"Sir, why do you hurt that cat?" asked Kauda.

"She's eaten my yogurt," said the man, "and I'm hungry."

"Leave the cat alone, and I'll pay you 100 rupees for the yogurt," said Kauda.

The man happily took the rupees, and Kauda continued down the road, with the cat following close behind him.

For several days, Kauda and the cat walked through the forests and climbed up steep mountain tracks. Then, one day, they came to another small village. There, Kauda saw a man hitting a little dog with a stick.

"Sir, why are you hitting this poor little dog?" asked Kauda.

"Because he won't stop barking," growled the man.

"I'll pay you 100 rupees if you let him go," said Kauda. The man happily took the rupees, and Kauda continued on his journey, with the cat and the dog following close behind.

For several more days, they walked along the tracks, passing old stone temples and Buddhas, until they came to another village. There, Kauda saw a man holding a mouse by its tail.

"Sir, why have you caught that little mouse?" asked Kauda.

"Because it eats my grain," grumbled the man.

"Set it free," said Kauda, "and I'll pay you 100 rupees."

The man gladly took the money and set the mouse free. Now Kauda had no money, but the cat and the dog and the mouse were his friends, and they walked happily on together.

Buddha   a carved figure in the likeness of the great leader Buddha

When it was night, Kauda and the animals lay down beside a pond to sleep. Suddenly, Kauda heard a voice coming from the pond.

"I have heard of your kindness to the animals," said the voice. "Take this magic shell. Throw it in the air and make a wish. It will be granted."

Kauda felt something pressed into his hand. It was a small shell. Kauda and the animals were hungry, so Kauda threw the shell into the air and said, "I wish for a bowl of rice for us to share."

Immediately, a large bowl of rice appeared in front of him. Kauda couldn't believe his eyes. Cat, Dog, Mouse, and Kauda ate until they were full. When they had finished eating, Kauda said to the animals, "Thank you for your company, my friends. Now I must go home to my father and share my good fortune with him. If any of you are ever in trouble, come to me, for I will always help you."

When Kauda arrived home, his father ran to greet him. He was delighted to see his son once more. Without wasting a moment, Kauda threw the magic shell into the air and said, "I wish to have a beautiful palace for my father."

At once, a glittering palace rose up before them. The old man could not believe his eyes.

The years passed, and Kauda grew into a handsome young man. He was very rich, but he was kind and always shared his riches with others.

One day, his father said, "Kauda, it is time you found someone to marry. I hear that the king has a beautiful daughter. I will go to the king and ask that she be allowed to marry you."

So the old man went to the royal palace to see the king. The king had heard about Kauda and his riches, and he agreed that his daughter could marry Kauda on one condition.

"Whoever marries my daughter must pave the street to my palace with gold," he said cunningly.

"Your wish shall be granted," said the old man.

cunning clever, especially at tricking people

Now one of the king's ministers heard this and was angry. He wanted his own son to marry the princess. He said to his son, "You must follow the old man and find out how Kauda makes his riches."

So the son disguised himself as a peddler and followed the old man through the city streets to Kauda's palace. He hid and watched as Kauda, following his father's instructions, fetched the magic shell and threw it into the air, saying, "I wish you to pave the street to the king's palace with gold."

Then Kauda put the shell under his pillow, climbed into bed, and soon fell asleep, dreaming of the beautiful princess.

The minister's son waited until he was sure Kauda was asleep. Then he crept to the bed, put his hand under the pillow, and stole the shell.

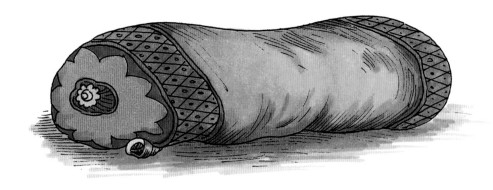

he greedy minister's son ran from Kauda's palace. When he was some distance away, he threw the shell into the air, shouting, "Take me and all Kauda's riches to a mountaintop, and bring the princess to me."

The wishing shell did as it was told.

When Kauda and his father awoke, they were back in their little wooden hut, and all their riches were gone. They were very despondent.

"I'll just have to go and seek my fortune again," Kauda said to his father bravely. So he set out down the trail.

despondent   discouraged and sad

Kauda walked for many days until, one day, he came upon his old friends Cat, Dog, and Mouse. They were very happy to see each other again. Kauda told them all that had happened to him since they had last been together.

Then he said, "I have grown tired of searching for my fortune. I think I'll go home to my father. He needs me, and I can help him, even if we are poor."

The animals were sorry for Kauda's misfortune. "We must try and help him as he helped us," they said. So the animals set out through the forests until they came to the mountains. On top of one of the mountains, they saw a palace glittering in the snow. "That must be Kauda's palace," they said, "and inside it must be the wishing shell." The animals began to climb higher and higher toward the palace.

When they reached the palace, Dog kept watch at the gates while Cat and Mouse slipped inside. They searched and searched until they found the minister's son. He was about to go to bed. As the animals hid and watched, he lay down and put the shell in his mouth. The animals looked at each other in dismay.

"I have a plan," whispered Mouse, "I will tickle his nose with my tail. When he sneezes, the shell will come flying out of his mouth. Cat, you must pick it up and run off." So Mouse crept up and tickled the nose of the minister's son, who let out a loud

"Achoo!"

The shell came flying out of his mouth. Cat picked it up in her mouth, and Mouse and Cat ran swiftly through the palace and back to the gate, where Dog was waiting.

dismay   an upset and worried way

The animals all raced down the mountain until they came to a wide river.

"How shall we cross?" cried Cat.

"Hop on my back," said Dog, "and I'll swim across."

So Mouse and Cat climbed onto Dog's back, but halfway across the river, Cat panicked. "We're going to drown!" cried Cat. As she spoke, the shell fell from her mouth into the river and was swallowed by a fish swimming by.

When they reached the other side, the animals looked at each other in despair. But then, unbelievably, an otter swam up with the fish in its mouth and tossed it onto the bank.

Cat was just about to grab the fish when a hawk swooped down and took it. The animals couldn't believe their bad luck.

despair   loss of all hope

Then Mouse said, "I have a plan. I will pretend to be dead, and the hawk will see me and fly down to grab me. Cat, you must catch the hawk and get it to spit out the fish."

So Mouse lay down on the river bank, and, sure enough, the hawk swooped down. Immediately, Cat pounced on the hawk while Dog cried, "Give up the fish, or Cat will kill you."

The hawk gave up the fish and flew off. Then Cat took the shell from the fish, and Dog dropped the fish back in the river.

For seven days and nights, the animals traveled down the mountains and through the forests, until they came to Kauda's village. Kauda was amazed to see his friends, and even more surprised when they presented him with the magic shell. He threw the shell into the air and said, "I wish for a bowl of rice for everyone."

The shell granted his wish.

As everyone shared the rice supper together, Kauda said, "My dear friends, you shall live with me and share my riches forever." Then Kauda threw the wishing shell high into the air and said, "I wish for my palace, my riches, and my princess to be returned to me."

On a mountaintop far away, the minister's son suddenly felt cold. The princess, who had been imprisoned all this time, found herself in a beautiful garden. A handsome young man was walking toward her. "I am Kauda," he said. "Will you marry me?"

"Thank you for rescuing me," said the princess. "I have heard of your kindness. I will be happy to marry you."

So Kauda and the princess were married and lived happily ever after. They always helped the poor who came to their door and shared their good fortune with their animal friends and others.

Discussion Starters

1   If you were Kauda and you saw animals being treated cruelly, would you have spent all your money to rescue them? If not, what would you have done instead?

2   Find the part in the story when Kauda decides to make the best of his life, even though he is poor. Do you think he and his father would have been happy even if the animals had not returned the magic shell?

Kauda took a risk when he showed compassion and kindness toward the animals in the story. In what ways do people in your life show compassion and kindness?